· AARON BLABEY ·

the BAD GUYS

COLLECTION
BOOKS #1-3

#1: THE BAD GUYS

#2: THE BAD GUYS IN
MISSION UNPLUCKABLE

#3: THE BAD GUYS IN THE
FURBALL STRIKES BACK

SCHOLASTIC INC.

TEXT AND ILLUSTRATIONS COPYRIGHT © 2015, 2016 BY AARON BLABEY

ALL RIGHTS RESERVED. PUBLISHED BY SCHOLASTIC INC., PUBLISHERS SINCE 1920, 557 BROADWAY,
NEW YORK, NY 10012. SCHOLASTIC AND ASSOCIATED LOGOS ARE TRADEMARKS AND/OR REGISTERED TRADEMARKS
OF SCHOLASTIC INC. THIS EDITION PUBLISHED UNDER LICENSE FROM SCHOLASTIC AUSTRALIA PTY LIMITED.
FIRST PUBLISHED BY SCHOLASTIC AUSTRALIA PTY LIMITED IN 2015, 2016.

THE PUBLISHER DOES NOT HAVE ANY CONTROL OVER AND DOES NOT ASSUME ANY
RESPONSIBILITY FOR AUTHOR OR THIRD-PARTY WEBSITES OF THEIR CONTENT.

NO PART OF THIS PUBLICATION MAY BE REPRODUCED, STORED IN A RETRIEVAL SYSTEM, OR TRANSMITTED IN ANY
FORM OR BY ANY MEANS, ELECTRONIC, MECHANICAL, PHOTOCOPYING, RECORDING, OR OTHERWISE, WITHOUT WRITTEN
PERMISSION OF THE PUBLISHER. FOR INFORMATION REGARDING PERMISSION, WRITE TO SCHOLASTIC AUSTRALIA, AN
IMPRINT OF SCHOLASTIC AUSTRALIA PTY LIMITED, 345 PACIFIC HIGHWAY, LINDFIELD, NSW 2070, AUSTRALIA.

THIS BOOK IS A WORK OF FICTION. NAMES, CHARACTERS, PLACES, AND INCIDENTS ARE EITHER THE PRODUCT OF
THE AUTHOR'S IMAGINATION OR ARE USED FICTITIOUSLY, AND ANY RESEMBLANCE TO ACTUAL PERSONS,
LIVING OR DEAD, BUSINESS ESTABLISHMENTS, EVENTS, OR LOCALES IS ENTIRELY COINCIDENTAL.

ISBN 978-1-338-62436-6

10 9 8 7 6 5 4 3 2   19 20 21 22 23

PRINTED IN THE U.S.A. 23
FIRST PRINTING 2019

· AARON BLABEY ·

the BAD GUYS

SCHOLASTIC INC.

GOOD DEEDS.

WHETHER YOU LIKE
IT OR NOT.

· CHAPTER 1 ·
MR. WOLF

Pssst!
Hey, you!

Yeah, you.

Get over here.

I said **GET OVER HERE**.

What's the problem?

Oh, I see.

Yeah, I get it . . .

You're thinking, "Ooooooh, it's a big, bad, scary wolf! I don't want to talk to him!

He's a **MONSTER**."

Well, let me tell you something, buddy –
Just because I've got

BIG POINTY TEETH and **RAZOR-SHARP CLAWS**

. . . and I *occasionally* like to dress up like an **OLD LADY**, that doesn't mean . . .

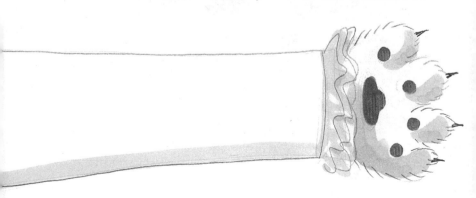

. . . I'm a

BAD GUY.

METROPOLITAN
POLICE DEPARTMENT

SUSPECT RAP SHEET

Name: Mr. Wolf

Case Number: 102 451A

Alias: Big Bad, Mr. Choppers, Grandma

Address: The Woods

Known Associates: None

Criminal Activity:

* Blowing down houses (the three pigs involved were too scared to press charges)

* Impersonating sheep

* Breaking into the homes of old women

* Impersonating old women

* Attempting to eat old women

* Attempting to eat relatives of old women

* Theft of night gowns and slippers

Status: Dangerous. DO NOT APPROACH.

It's all **LIES**, I tell you.

But you don't believe me, do you?

Because I'm the Bad Guy, right?

I'm a great guy. A *nice* guy, even.

But I'm not just talking about **ME** . . .

I've got some buddies who have the same problem, so I've asked them to join us.

Any minute now, they'll be walking right through that door.

They're great guys. But just like me, they are **MISUNDERSTOOD**.

So don't go anywhere, OK?

· CHAPTER 2 ·
THE GANG

OK. Are you ready
to learn the truth?

You'd better be, baby.

Let's see who's here,
shall we?

Heeey! Look who it is!
It's my good pal,

MR. SNAKE.

You're going to *love* him.
He's a real . . .

. . . sweetheart.

METROPOLITAN POLICE DEPARTMENT

SUSPECT RAP SHEET

Name: Mr. Snake

Case Number: 354 22C

Alias: The Chicken Swallower

Address: Unknown

Known Associates: None

Criminal Activity: * Broke into Mr. Ho's Pet Store

* Ate all the mice at Mr. Ho's Pet Store

* Ate all the canaries at Mr. Ho's Pet Store

* Ate all the guinea pigs at Mr. Ho's Pet Store

* Tried to eat Mr. Ho at Mr. Ho's Pet Store

* Tried to eat the doctor who tried to save Mr. Ho

* Tried to eat the policemen who tried to
  save the doctor who tried to save Mr. Ho

* Ate the police dog who tried to save the
  policemen who tried to save the doctor
  who tried to save Mr. Ho

Status: Very dangerous. DO NOT APPROACH.

Look at this face!
Is this the face of a monster?

I don't think so.

This is **ONE SWEET GUY**.

Will this take long, man?
I've got mice to eat.

HAHA
HAHA!

What a joker this guy is!

"I've got mice to eat!"
That's a good one.

What a wise guy.

HA HA HA.

HA.

HA.

Goodness,
I wonder who could be
at the door?

Well, well. If it isn't
MR. PIRANHA.

Now, if anyone has
a bad reputation,
it's this guy . . .

Hola.

METROPOLITAN POLICE DEPARTMENT

SUSPECT RAP SHEET

Name: Mr. Piranha

Case Number: 775 906T

Alias: The Butt Biter

Address: Tropical Rivers

Known Associates: The Piranha Brothers Gang, 900,543 members, all related to Mr. Piranha

Criminal Activity:

* Eating tourists

Status: EXTREMELY dangerous. DO NOT APPROACH.

What's *he* doing here?
That guy is crazy . . .

SHHH!

Hey, Mr. P!
I know a sweet guy
like you wouldn't say
no to a cupcake . . .

I've come all the way from Bolivia, *hermanos.*

And I'm hungry! So where's the

MEAT?

HA HA!

These guys are killing me! Always with the jokes!

No meat. Just cake.

I'm

HUNGRY.

You got any seals?

METROPOLITAN POLICE DEPARTMENT

SUSPECT RAP SHEET

Name: Mr. Shark

Case Number: 666 885E

Alias: Jaws

Address: Popular Tourist Destinations

* Will literally eat ANYTHING or ANYBODY.

RIDICULOUSLY DANGEROUS. RUN!
SWIM! DON'T EVEN READ THIS!
Status: GET OUT OF HERE!!

See?! This is what I'm talking about!
How will anyone take us seriously as

GOOD GUYS

if all you want to do is

EAT EVERYONE?

What am I **TALKING** about?
Well, sit down and I'll explain.

And that means *you*, too.

· CHAPTER 3 ·
the
GOOD GUYS
CLUB

AAAAHHHHHHH!!!!!!

Typical . . .

Hey, shouldn't you two be in water?

I'll be
wherever
I want.

Got it?

Me too, *chico*.

See? This is why
I don't work with fish.

Because **THIS** is the very first meeting of . . .

THE
GOOD
GUYS
CLUB!

That's right!

The
GOOD
GUYS
CLUB!

I beg your pardon?

You heard me.

Aren't you tired of being the
VILLAIN?

Aren't you tired of the
SCREAMS?

Aren't you tired of the
FEAR?

Not particularly.

Not in the
slightest.

OF COURSE YOU ARE!

And I have the solution!

POP QUIZ!

Let's say we find a cat stuck in a tree.

What do we do?

This guy's *loco*.

No, I'm not!
I'm a **GENIUS!**
And I'm going to make us all
HEROES!

He's completely lost his mind.

I came all the way from Bolivia for THIS?

You'll be glad you did, Mr. Piranha.

And so will you, Mr. Shark.

This is going to be **AWESOME**.

Now, everybody climb aboard!

And let's go do some

GOOD!

· CHAPTER 4 ·
CRUISING FOR TROUBLE

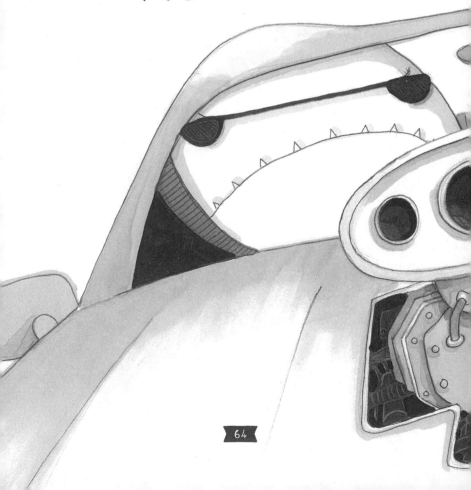

This car is a fuel-injected, **200-HORSEPOWER**, rock 'n' rollin' chariot of flaming **COOLNESS**, my friend. If we're going to be good guys, don't you think we should **LOOK GOOD**, too?

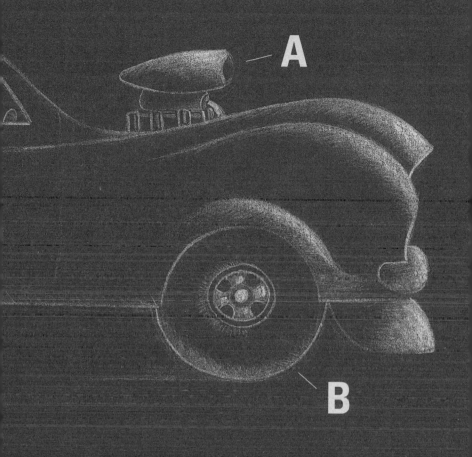

A - Wicked powerful V8 engine that runs on undiluted panther pee.

B - Fat wheels for just looking insanely cool.

C - Custom ejector seats for personal safety and also practical jokes.

D - Oversized muffler for being very, very loud at all times.

And it's roomy, too!

Hey, it's a sweet ride, *chico*. But I get carsick, man. So, what ARE we doing out here?

We're looking for trouble, my friend. If we're going to be heroes, we **ALWAYS** need to be on the lookout for trouble . . .

We need to
be able to
SMELL
trouble!

In fact . . . wait a second . . .
I think I can smell trouble
right now . . .

HEY!

What's the **big deal**, *chico*?
Car travel makes me
let off a little **gas**.

SO WHAT?

GOOD**BOY**

Actually, that feels real nice.

Seriously though, man . . . what are we looking for?

SCREEECH!

THAT is what we're looking for, Mr. Snake!

Meow!

BINGO!

· CHAPTER 5 ·
HERE, KITTY

So, what are we going to do?

Rescue the cat.

And what are we **NOT** going to do?

Eat the cat.

THAT'S RIGHT!
I don't know about you, but I feel PUMPED!

OK, now let's do this thing . . .

What was *that*? Are you trying to give him a heart attack?

WHAT? I was, like, being totally cool . . .

Let me handle this.

HEY, YOU! Get down here, or I'll **SHIMMY** up that tree and **BITE** you on your **FURRY LITTLE BUTT!**

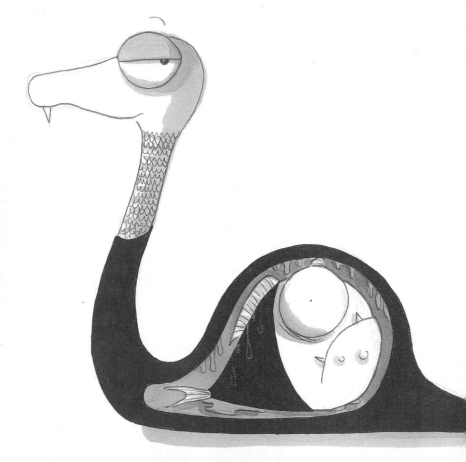

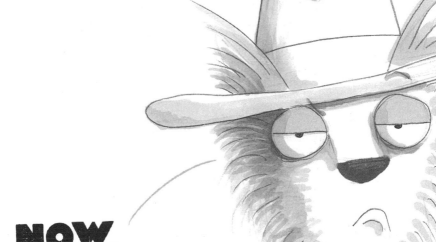

NOW,

please don't be alarmed.

It's true,

snakes can be tricky and they do tend to

swallow whatever they like.

BUT – luckily, they swallow things *whole*

and I happen to know a gentle,

harmless technique that'll fix this right up.

Excuse me for one moment . . .

¡Ay, caramba!

SPLURT!

• CHAPTER 6 •
THE PLAN

Nice work.
High fives,
all around!

You're the only
one with hands.

Our first mission.

It's time for

OPERATION DOG POUND!

THE

534 10

200 DOG'

DOG POUND

20 GUARDS

ONE WAY IN.
ONE WAY OUT.

IRON BARS!
RAZOR WIRE!
BAD FOOD!

There are **200** puppies locked up in the

MAXIMUM SECURITY CITY DOG POUND.

Their hopes and dreams are trapped
behind walls of stone and bars of steel.

But guess what?

We're going to **SET THEM FREE!**

We couldn't get a kitten out of a tree. How are we supposed to bust out 200 dogs?

It's easy! One of us just has to get in there and open the cages!

And how do we do that?

Are you going to dress up like an old lady AGAIN? It doesn't work, man. You ALWAYS get caught!

Who said anything about *me*?

· CHAPTER 7 ·
THE POUND

Hello?
Oh, certainly, miss.
I'll buzz you in.

Now, what can I do
for . . . uh . . . you?

I'm just a pretty young lady who has lost her dog.
Please, oh please, can you help me, sir?

Well,
OF COURSE!

Anything for such
a lovely young lady.

Cool.

He's in!
I **KNEW** this
would work.

Now, you know what to do.
Once those cages are open,
we won't have long,
so don't mess it up.

Climb aboard, fellas!

What's that
thing for?

Never mind. Just hold on tight.
And remember — once Mr. Shark
gives me the signal, I'll get you
inside and all you have to do is tell
the dogs which way to run.

GOT IT?

Yeah. But
how do we
get inside?

But don't worry!

I have **EXCELLENT** aim

and I'm **85%** sure

that I'll get you in on my first throw —

THAT'S

how confident I am!

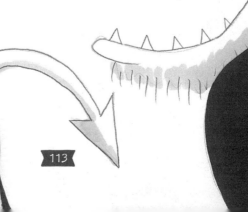

Well, here's the last cage.
Is THIS your dog?

NO! Oh, woe is me!
I shall never find
my dog!

OH,
BOO HOO!
BOO
HOO!

There's no time to talk! Hold on tight, little buddies.

It's time . . .

OK.
Best out of three.

YEAH.
I'm getting the
hang of it now . . .

SPLAT!

If we survive this, I'm going to *eat* that wolf.

WHOOOSH!

Not if I do first.

It worked!

OK,
MR. WOLF . . .
HIT IT!

I hear you,
little buddy.
REV! REV!

Let's give those puppies their . . .

· CHAPTER 8 ·
SO, HOW ABOUT IT?

I'm not a SARDINE! I'M A PIRANHA, man! **PIRANHA!**

Whatever.

You're missing the point, guys. **WE DID IT!** We gave 200 dogs a whole new life. Doesn't that make you feel **AWESOME?!**

You really do hug WAY more than I'm comfortable with, man.

Aw, **C'MON!**

You loved it! I KNOW you did!

Tell me the truth — didn't it feel great

to be the **GOOD GUY** for once?

Tell me how it felt, fellas . . .

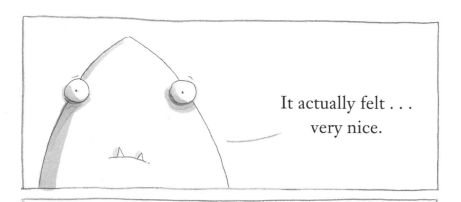

It actually felt . . .
very nice.

It felt better than nice.
It felt . . . good.

It felt **WONDERFUL**,
man. But they still called me
a SARDINE!!!

If you stick with me, little buddy, no one will ever mistake you for a sardine ever again! You'll be Bolivia's most famous hero! Are you with me?

Sure. But you'd better be right, *chico*.

And what about you, big fella?

I . . . I really liked being good. I'm in.

That just leaves you, handsome. What do you say? Want to be in my gang?

Only if I have your word that there'll be no more hugging.

I'll try, baby! But I'm not making any promises!

Today is the first day of our **new** lives.

We are **not** Bad Guys anymore.

WE'RE
GOOD GUYS!

And we are going to make the
world a **better** place.

For the first time in my life
. . . the future smells sweet!

Wait a second —

That doesn't
smell sweet . . .

Piranha, did
you fart *again*?

I get gassy when I'm
upset. Just deal with
it, *chico*.

TO BE CONTINUED . . .

• AARON BLABEY •

the BAD GUYS

in

MISSION
UNPLUCKABLE

SCHOLASTIC INC.

PANIC AT THE DOG POUND!

We interrupt this program to bring you a breaking news story.

TIFFANY FLUFFIT

is our reporter on the scene. Tiffany, what can you tell us?

CHUCK MELON

Thanks, Chuck!

Well, there have been **SHOCKING** scenes at the **DOG POUND** today.

It seems some kind of **CRAZED GANG** burst in, smashed down a wall, and then drove away in a very loud hot-rod car, causing **200 TERRIFIED PUPPY DOGS** to run away in fright.

TIFFANY FLUFFIT 6 NEWS

I have with me **MR. GRAHAM PLONKER**,
Chief of Dog Pound Security.

Mr. Plonker, how would you describe these
MONSTERS?

Uh . . . well . . . it all happened so
fast, but . . . I'm pretty sure there
were four of them . . .

I mean, there was definitely a **WOLF**.

EXCLUSIVE FOOTAGE!

A really *mean*-looking wolf, with pointy teeth.

And there was a **SNAKE**.

HAVE YOU SEEN THIS SNAKE?

A very *ugly* snake, who also seemed very cranky for some reason . . .

Uh, then there was a **YOUNG LADY** . . .

PRETTY GIRL? OR DEADLY SHARK?

. . . or possibly a gigantic **SHARK**. It was hard to tell which . . .

Oh yeah, and there was also some kind of nasty little fish.

MUTANT SARDINE ON THE LOOSE!

Maybe a **SARDINE**.

Not sure.

But, Mr. Plonker, would
   you say that these
   villains seemed . . .

DANGEROUS?

Oh yes, Tiffany. They're
dangerous, all right.

In fact, I'd say we are dealing
with some *serious* . . .

LIVE FROM THE DOG POUND 6 NEWS

CHAPTER 1
OK, LET'S TRY THAT AGAIN

What's that guy talking about?
We **SAVED** those puppy dogs!
It was a
RESCUE!
We're the **GOOD GUYS** here!

AND FOR THE LAST TIME,
I AM **NOT** A SARDINE!
I'M A
PIRANHA!

MUNCH! MUNCH! MUNCH!

See, Wolf? No one is **EVER** going to believe we're good guys. I'm getting out of here before the cops come looking for us.

Oh, **NO** you don't, Mr. Snake! We're not going to quit now. We're just getting started.

Don't forget **HOW GOOD** it felt to rescue those dogs!

All we need to do now is make sure that everyone can **SEE** that we're **HEROES**.

We just need to do something **SO AWESOME** that the whole world will sit up and take notice!

What did you have in mind, Mr. Wolf?

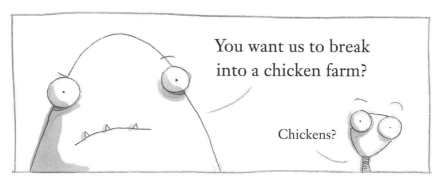

Well, take a look INSIDE
Sunnyside Chicken Farm, fellas.

10,000 CHICKENS!

Stuffed into **TINY** cages!

24 hours a day!

With **NO** sunlight!

And **NO** room to run and play!

But that's awful!
That's the worst thing
I've ever heard!

What are we waiting for?!

WE NEED TO SET THOSE
LITTLE CHICKIE-BABIES
FREE!

Let's go! Let's go! Let's go!
Let's go! Let's go! Let's go!
Let's go! Let's go! Let's go!
Let's go! Let's go! Let's go!

LET'S GO!

Well, *hellooooo . . .*

Are you OK, man?

Huh?

DROOL

Oh yeah . . . sorry.
I was just thinking that chickens are delicious—I mean, *DELIGHTFUL*—and I think we need to save them all **RIGHT NOW**.

Oh, if only it were that simple, my friend.
But I'm afraid I have some bad news . . .

Sunnyside Chicken Farm is **IMPOSSIBLE** to break into!

It's a **MAXIMUM SECURITY CHICKEN FARM** with **STEEL WALLS** that are 30 feet high and 8 feet thick!

There are **NO WINDOWS** and all the doors are **HEAVILY GUARDED.**

SUNNYSIDE INC.

And even if you *did* get inside, you'd be caught
instantly because . . .

If you touch the FLOOR, an **ALARM** goes off!
If you touch the WALLS, an **ALARM** goes off!

And if you walk into the LASER BEAMS,
an **ALARM** goes off!

- FLOOR ALARMS
- WALL ALARMS
- LASER ALARMS

Did you say
LASER BEAMS?
Why are you even showing us
this, *chico*? We don't have the
skills to pull off a job like this!

No, we don't.
But I know a guy who does.

Who?

the FREAKY GEEK

Hey, dudes! It's totally awesome to meet you!

Aieeeeee!
RUN *CHICOS*! It's a
TARANTULA!!!

I'm sorry about this, Legs. I don't know what's wrong with them.

Aw, it's cool. Happens all the time.

LEGS?!

You *know* this monster?!

What were you thinking, bringing a tarantula into our clubhouse?

. . . Can't breathe . . .
spider . . .
Mommy . . .
Mommy . . .
I want my mommy . . .

Mr. Shark! Pull yourself together!
You guys should be ASHAMED of yourselves!
LEGS is just like us.
He's a GOOD GUY with a BAD reputation.

Aw, thanks,
Wolfie.

He's **DANGEROUS,** man.

Yeah!
And why isn't he
wearing any pants?

I don't do pants, dude. I like to feel free.

. . . can't breathe . . .
no pants . . .
freaking . . . out . . .

Okeydoke.

Legs? Why don't you
show them what you can do?

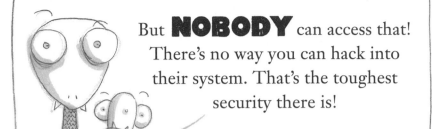

But **NOBODY** can access that! There's no way you can hack into their system. That's the toughest security there is!

Yeah, it *is* kind of tricky.

TAP! TAP! TAP! TAP! TAP! TAP! TAP! TAP!

But it's worth it just to see you smile, Mr. Snake.

Ta-da!

That's
IMPOSSIBLE!

Not for a **SUPERHACKER** like Legs! He's a computer **GENIUS**. And he has a plan that will get us inside that chicken farm.

Thanks, Wolfie. But first, I'd better put this back the way I found it. We are good guys, after all . . .

. . . and I wouldn't like to get us in trouble. Sorry, Mr. Snake. You're *dangerous* again, I'm afraid.

Hey!

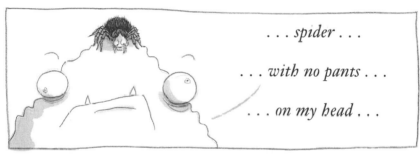

· CHAPTER 3 ·
MISSION, LIKE, TOTALLY IMPOSSIBLE

OK, dudes, I took your advice and found myself some clothes. What do you think?

I can still see his **BIG FURRY BUTT.**

Cut it out, Piranha. Just listen to him.

OK.

To get you guys inside Sunnyside Chicken Farm, all I need to do is hack into their main computer and switch off all the alarms.

BUT

there's a problem . . .

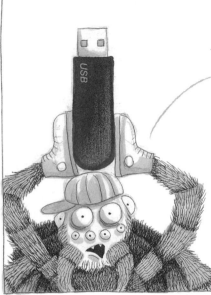

The security is **SO HIGH** that I can't do it from here.

I need you guys to plug **THIS THING** into their computer, so I can access it.

Once you do that, I can SHUT IT ALL DOWN and get you to those chickens.

Wait a minute. You're telling us that you can hack into my police file, but you **CAN'T** get into a CHICKEN FARM without our help?

Yeah. It's WEIRD.
This is one SCARY
chicken farm, dude.

But if it's so scary, how do we
get to the computer?
Wolf said there's no way into
the building!

Well, there is **ONE** way.

But it sure isn't easy . . .

There's a
SMALL HATCH
on the roof.

You'll need to go
through the hatch
and **DROP**
150 feet on a rope
to the computer
below. Once you
get to it, **JUST
PLUG ME IN**.

BUT!

If you touch the
WALLS or the
FLOOR, the
ALARMS will
go off and you'll
get caught.

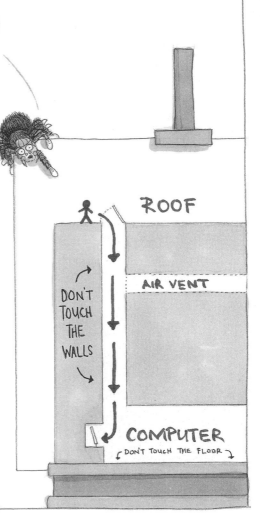

That's it?
That doesn't sound so bad.

I'm not finished.

Once you plug me in, you have to climb back up the rope, crawl through this **AIR VENT** and follow the tunnel to the CHICKEN CAGES.

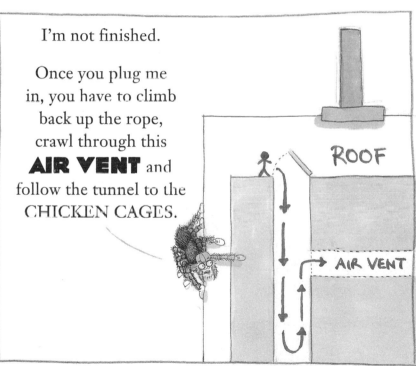

ROOF

AIR VENT

Like I said, that doesn't
sound so bad.

I'M STILL NOT FINISHED.

You see, before you reach the chicken cages,
you'll come to the **LASER BEAMS**.
And if you touch one, the alarms will go off.

Oh, and they'll zap you.
And they *really* hurt.

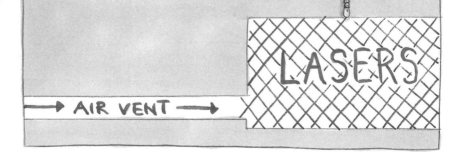

→ AIR VENT →

LASERS

But why are the lasers still on?
I thought you were going to shut
down all the alarms.

I will.
The **OTHER** alarms will be off.

But the **LASER ALARMS**
can only be turned off by hand.
You have to flick a switch
once you're inside.

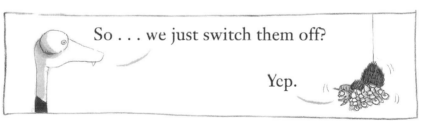

So . . . we just switch them off?

Yep.

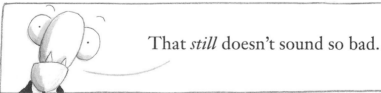

That *still* doesn't sound so bad.

That's because I'm **STILL NOT FINISHED!**

The switch is on the OTHER SIDE of the laser beams, so you have to GO **THROUGH** THEM to reach it!

CHICKENS THIS WAY

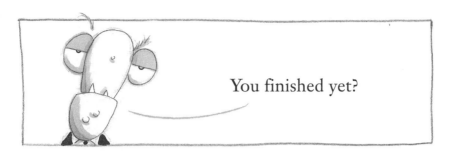

You finished yet?

Uhhh . . . yep.

Good! Because that sounds **LOCO!** There's **NO WAY** we can pull this off, man!

Oh yes, we can!

But **ONLY** if we work as a **TEAM!**

So, Snake and Piranha—
you guys are coming with ME!

We are going to **GET INSIDE**,

plug **THIS THING** into the computer, and

GET TO THOSE CHICKENS!

This is going to be

GREAT!

But . . . what about me?

You're going to be working with me, Big Guy.
It's OUR JOB to get these guys in and out of there safely!
Isn't this awesome? You and I are going to SPEND A
LOT OF TIME TOGETHER!

*Oh . . . that's . . .
great . . . but . . .
I think . . .
I'm going . . .
to cry . . .*

No time for tears, Mr. Shark.

WE'VE GOT CHICKENS TO SAVE!

· CHAPTER 4 ·
DOWN THE HATCH

Hey, what are you guys doing
all the way over there?

LATER THAT NIGHT . . .

SUNNYSIDE
CHICKEN FARM
KEEP OUT!

We look ridiculous.

SUNNYSIDE
INC.

Hey, Tarantula! What's with the stupid suits?

Shhh! Not so loud, Mr. Piranha. These suits are GREAT! They'll keep you cool and make you really hard to spot.

PLUS!

Each suit has a microphone and earpiece, so we can all talk to each other.

GOT IT?

Hey, Wolf, do you really promise there'll be chickens down there?

It's a **CHICKEN** FARM! Of course there'll be chickens. Why are you so worried about that?

Oh, no reason.

I just really **LOVE** chickens, man.

They're so nice to eat—I mean, they're so nice to *MEET*.

Yeah . . .

 You DO understand that we're here to SAVE the chickens, don't you?

 Uh-huh.

 And you wouldn't try to **EAT** any chickens, would you?

 Uh-uh.

 Hey! Can we just DO THIS? My jumpsuit is chafing.

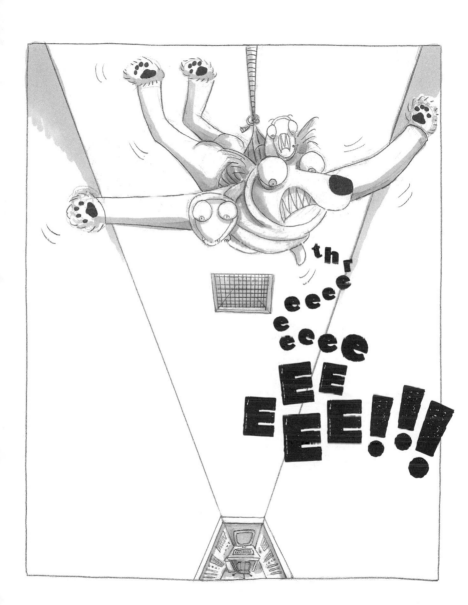

OK. OK. OK. Well, the walls are a *little* closer than I expected.

Mr. Shark! Whatever you do, make sure you lower us *SLOWLY*.

I hear you.

Do you need a hand, Big Buddy?

BOING!

EEEEEEEEE

FOOF!

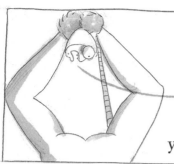

Whoa. That was close.

¡AY, CARAMBA!

Mr. Wolf?
Has anyone ever told you that
your face looks like a **BUTT?**

What?

Oh. Sorry. My mistake.

Hey, look! The computer!
I think I can reach it . . .

He didn't see us.
Why didn't he see us?

Shhh! I don't know.
He must have really bad eyesight.
Um . . . OK . . .
Any suggestions on what we do now?

Are you kidding?
WE GET
OUT OF
HERE!
SHARK?!
ABORT!
ABORT!
PULL US
UP NOW!

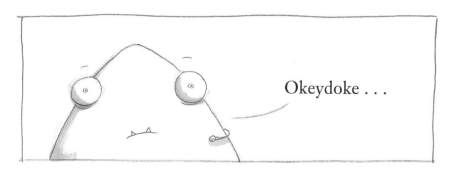

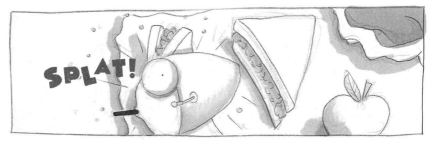

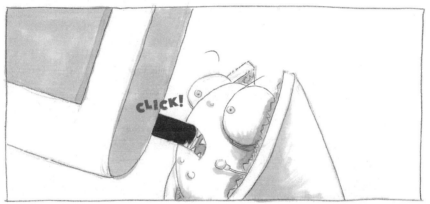

This was a one-way ticket, *chico.*

WHAT? We can't just leave you behind!

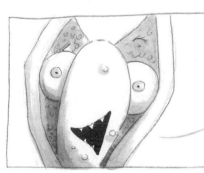

You have to, *hermanos.*
There is no other way.

Go and save those little
chickens, man.
Save them for **ME!**

Wolf! Snap out of it!
SHARK! Pull us up!

You got it.

Hurry up, man.
Just get in the vent, will you?

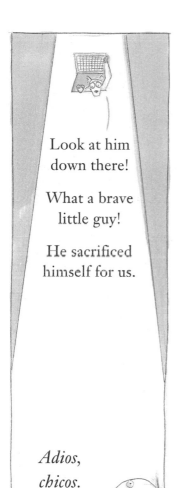

Look at him down there!

What a brave little guy!

He sacrificed himself for us.

Adios, chicos.

Yeah, yeah. Let's do this. I'm starving—I mean, I'm *STARTING* to want to save some chickens. Yep.

You're right. We should go.

Adios, Mr. Piranha.

Stay safe.

Easy for you to say, baby.

· CHAPTER 5 ·
MIND THE GAP

See, Mr. Snake?
This is what I've been talking about—without Mr. Piranha, we would **NEVER** have made it this far. **THAT'S** what being on a team is all about.
COOPERATION.

Yeah, yeah, yeah, that's *so* interesting, but WHERE ARE THE CHICKENS, man?

Just up ahead, I'd say.

This bit has been a lot easier than I thought. I really don't know what all the fuss was ab—

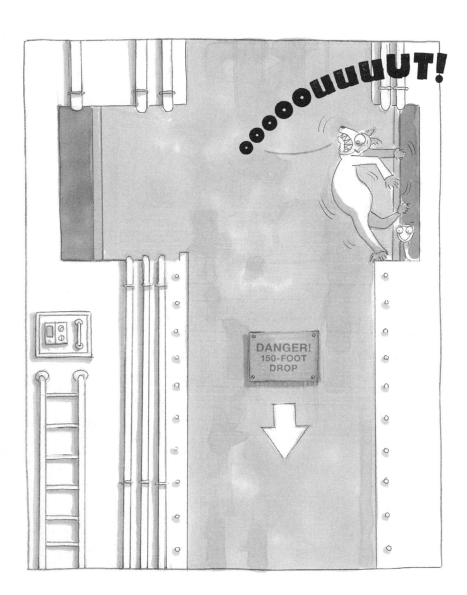

Hey! I have an idea.
Why don't you stay here?

I'll go and eat—
I mean, *GREET*
those chickens.

Noooo! I'm slipping!
I . . . can't hold on.
You have to . . . help me . . .

Really?
That's a bit annoying.

ANNOYING?!
IF YOU DON'T HELP ME,
I'M GOING TO **DIE!**

You need to go on a diet, man. You really do.

Now, let's think.

What do we do?

We're trapped.

It's not just ME that's trapped. And it's not just YOU. It's **US**.

We're trapped as a **TEAM**. So we need to get out of this as a **TEAM**.

I'VE **GOT** IT!

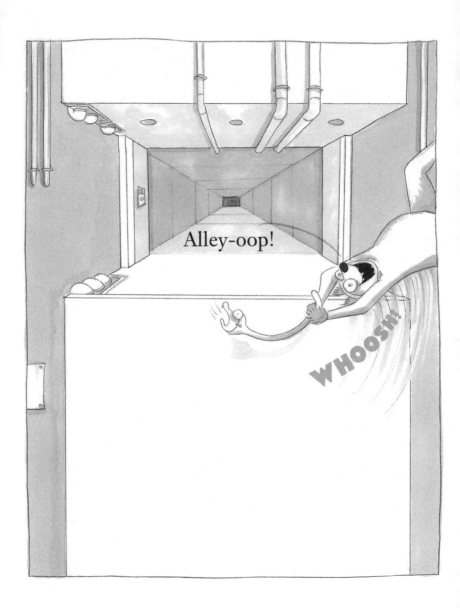

· CHAPTER 6 ·
LET'S START OVER

That's not good.

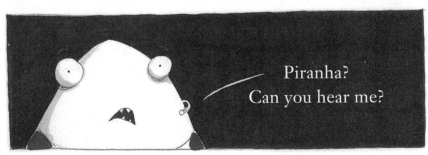

Piranha?
Can you hear me?

Mr. Shark? Is that you?

I'm about to be a monkey's lunch here, man.

You sit tight, Mr. P. I'm coming to get you.

BOING!

Can I help, **BIG FELLA?**

Really . . . scared . . . of . . . spiders . . .

Uh-huh. And why is that?
It's OK, you can tell me.

OK, well . . .

you're **FREAKY** to look at because

you have **TOO MANY EYES** and

TOO MANY LEGS

and I'm SO creeped

out by you that

**I MIGHT
THROW UP!**

But . . . I'm sorry if that
sounds rude.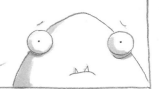

 It's OK.

No, really. I feel terrible saying
that. You must think I'm awful.

 No, that's OK.
You seem like a nice guy.
But can I ask you one little thing?

Yes, of course.

Well . . .

since I can't help being a tarantula in the same way

that you CAN'T HELP BEING A

MASSIVE, TERRIFYING SEA MONSTER,

I wonder
if you could just

GET OVER IT

and then

MAYBE

I could help you rescue
your friend!

Um . . . OK.

I'm so sorry. That was really uncool.

It's OK. That's good advice.

Well . . . um . . . how are we going to rescue that piranha?

I've heard you're pretty good at disguises. Is that right?

I have my moments.

OK, well, I'm REALLY good at making stuff. So why don't we work together?

OK.

But what kind of disguise is going to get me inside a chicken farm?

Why don't you pull the feathers out of those pillows there, Mr. Shark, and I'll tell you my idea.

· CHAPTER 7 ·
TRUST ME, I'M A SNAKE

Oh no! Look at those laser beams! I'll **NEVER** get through!

I think we have a problem.

CAGE ➡

Oooooh no, no, no, no. There's no problem—I'll fit through those lasers. I'll just have to handle this one **ALONE.**

Are you sure?

Oh, ABSOLUTELY. I'll just wriggle my way across and have a chicken feast—I mean . . . I'll get those chickens **RELEASED.**

Yeah.
Released.
Heh heh.

But you'll switch off the lasers when you get across?

Yeah, yeah, sure.

GO BE
A HERO,
MR.
SNAKE!

YOU **MADE** IT!

You're amazing!

Now, just switch off the lasers so I can get across . . .

Hmmm, sure.

Just give me a few minutes to find the switch . . .

 You take your time, little buddy!

YOU ROCK!

 I'm just SO proud of these guys.

♪ ♫

WHISTLE
WHISTLE

 Geez, it's been fifteen minutes.

Are you OK over there, Mr. Snake?

Aha! He's done it.

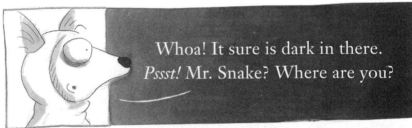

Whoa! It sure is dark in there.
Pssst! Mr. Snake? Where are you?

Oh, there you are!
Is everything OK?

Urghugh.

Mr. Snake?

What arc you doing over there?

In the dark?

Behind all those . . . **EMPTY** cages?

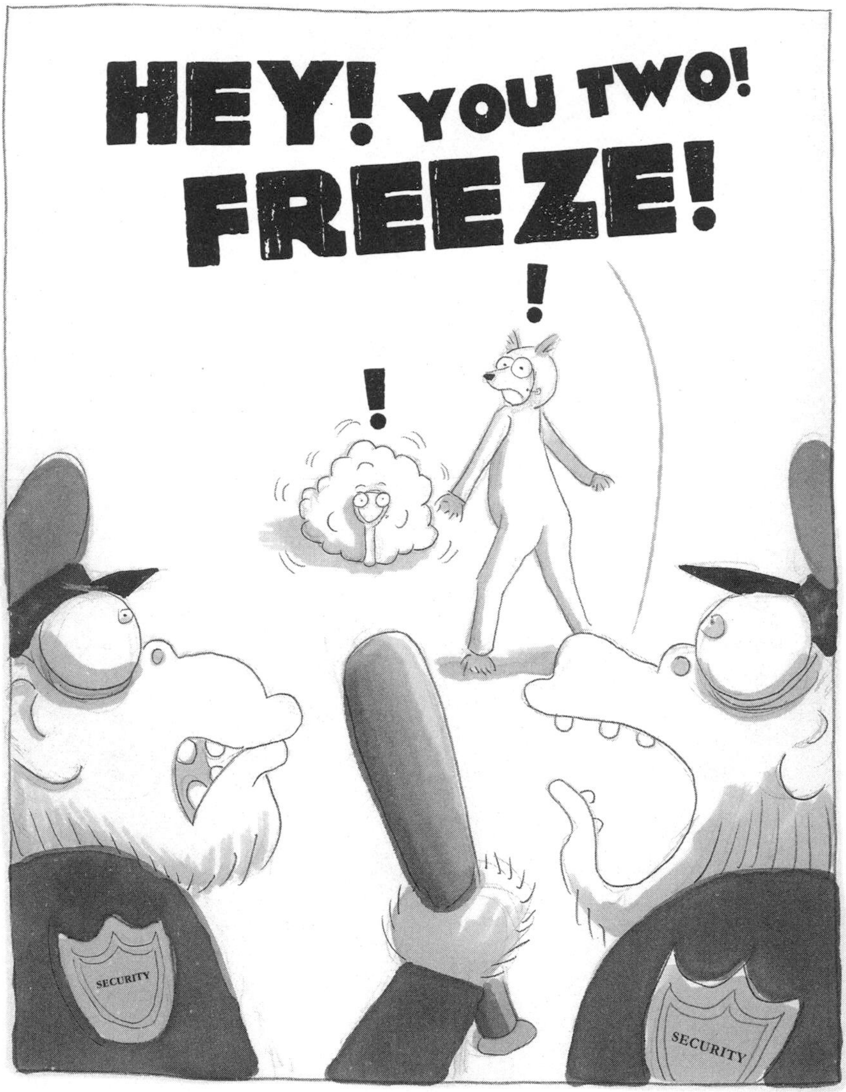
HEY! YOU TWO! FREEZE!
!
!
SECURITY
SECURITY

Oh, I don't think so.

Snake, you are *not* going to ruin this plan. No, you are not.

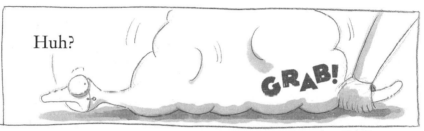

Huh?

GRAB!

NO.
YOU.
ARE.
NOT.

· CHAPTER 8 ·
WHOLE LOTTA CHICKEN

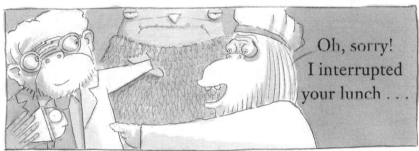

 Wow! I barely recognized you.

 Yeah, I know.
I'm good at disguises.

WHOOP! WHOOP! WHOOP!

OH NO! They've set off the alarm!

WHOOP! WHOOP! WHOOP!

But Wolf and Snake will be trapped!

Guys! It's Legs! Get out of there! They're coming for you!

WHOOP! WHOOP! WHOOP!

We're not leaving without our *chicos*.

Or our chickens.

253

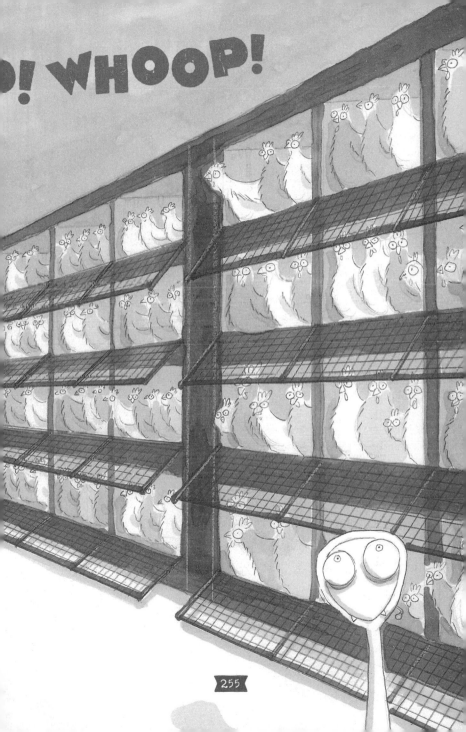

We've opened the cages, but they won't run. What's wrong with these stupid chickens?

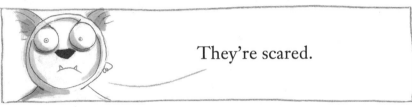

They're scared.

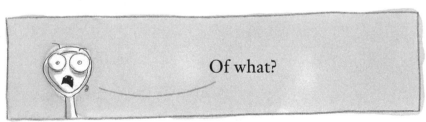

Of what?

OF THE CREEP WHO TRIED TO **EAT THEM!**

I couldn't help it.

I'm sorry.

Yeah, well, "sorry" won't help us now, Mr. Snake.

What are we going to do? The chickens are terrified.

They need someone to **FOLLOW**.

They need someone to **TRUST**.

They need . . .

Wow. That's one big chicken.

All right, girls. I know you're scared, but this is your **ONE CHANCE** to get out of this horrible place.

Do you understand?

Run, little chickies! Run!

THEN LET'S GET OUT OF HERE!

Mr. Piranha!
You're here!

Are you OK?

I'm completely coated
in mayonnaise.

Oh. I see.

It's not too bad, actually.

I kind of like it.

Throw me at him! It's your only chance!

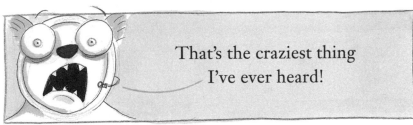

That's the craziest thing I've ever heard!

This is my chance to do some good, Mr. Wolf.

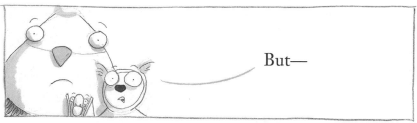

THROW ME NOW OR THESE CHICKENS WILL NEVER BE FREE!

DO IT!

And don't miss.

GOT IT?

Got it.

Hi. Let's play a game. The first person to open the door doesn't get bitten by a snake.

You win.

Now, can I ask you to please lock all the guards in behind us after we leave?

Yes, we do.

Oh, and if you don't, I **WILL** find out where you live and you **WILL** find me in your bed in the middle of the night.

Do we have a deal?

Marvelous!

BOING!

See? You're not the only Good Guy around here . . .

I knew it! I knew it! I knew it!

OK. Less hugs. More escaping.

· CHAPTER 9 ·
WHAT A TEAM

I am so proud of you guys! **10,000** chickens are free because of **YOU!**

I think we're starting to get the hang of this hero thing, fellas.

And that means you, too, Mr. Snake.

OK, Huggy Bear. Let's not make a great big hairy deal out of it.

Aw, sure thing, you old grouch! Let's get out of here . . .

But . . .

What happened to the **CAR?!**

Oh yeah. While I was waiting for you guys to get back, I fitted it with **MONSTER TRUCK** tires and a **JET ENGINE**. I hope you don't mind?

We don't mind!

And I noticed that you seemed a little cramped in there, Mr. Shark, so I've modified your seat. If you don't like it, I can always put it back the way it was.

I . . . I *love* it, Legs. You're very thoughtful.

Thank you.

Anytime, Mr. Shark. Anytime at all.

*I'm breathing.
It's all good.
I'm breathing
It's all good.
I'm breathing.
It's all good.*

SQUEAK!

Hey! Did anybody else hear that?

Nope. My mistake.
There's nothing here. It's empty.

Well, no. It's not
completely empty . . .

Look!

Awww! Look at the widdle guinea pig! What are you doing here all alone?

I think he's named Marmalade. Cute, isn't he?

MARMALADE

Well, Marmalade—we are the

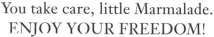

GOOD GUYS CLUB.

And we have come to set you free!

You take care, little Marmalade. ENJOY YOUR FREEDOM!

See you, little guy.

Good . . . guys?

GOOD GUYS?

And just because they call themselves
GOOD GUYS, they think they can

BREAK INTO MY CHICKEN FARM AND SET MY CHICKENS FREE?!

AND THEY THINK THEY CAN
GET AWAY WITH IT?

Well, we'll see about that. I shall make them pay.

Oh yes . . .

I SHALL MAKE THEM PAY! HEHEHEHEHE! HEHEHEHE!

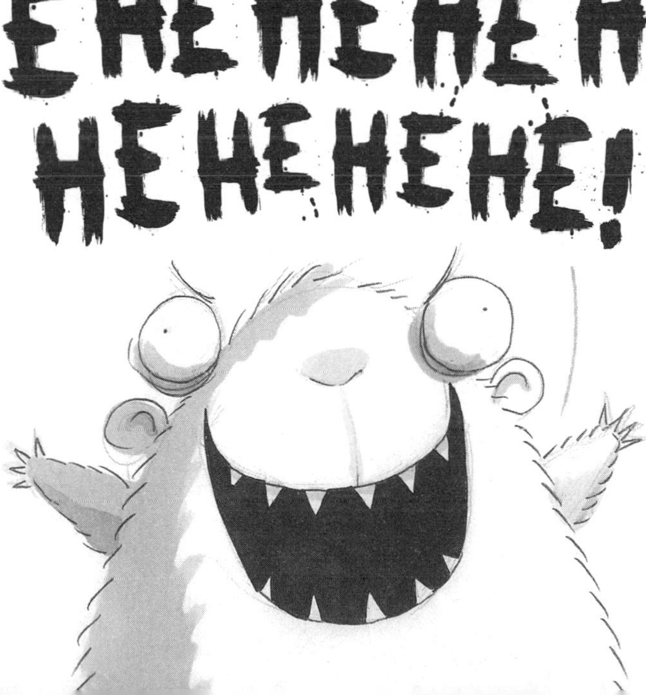

AARON BLABEY

the BAD GUYS

in

THE FURBALL STRIKES BACK

SCHOLASTIC INC.

HEROES OR VILLAINS?

A SPECIAL REPORT BY

TIFFANY FLUFFIT NEWS

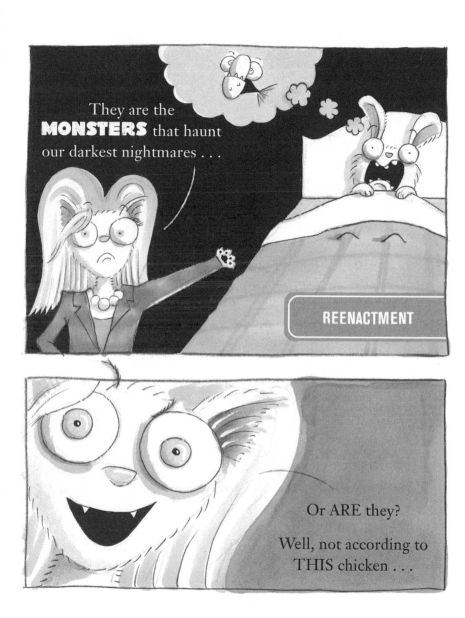

289

SUNNYSIDE CHICKEN FARM was a terrible place. We spent our whole lives locked in tiny cages. But then that wonderful wolf and his friends—they set us free!

BROOKE

But . . . didn't one of them try to EAT you?

Yes. But he spat me back out again.

IS THIS CHICKEN *CRAZY*?

And Brooke is not the only one to claim that these VILLAINS are actually . . .

HEROES IN DISGUISE!

Every one of the 10,000 chickens set free from Sunnyside has told the same story.

POLICE REPORT

Sunnyside

SHOULD MUTANT SARDINES BE ALLOWED TO WALK THE STREETS?

I thought they were lovely.
Especially the really big chicken.
Or maybe he was a shark.
It was hard to tell . . .

PAT, HOMEMAKER

They inspired me to
follow my dreams.
I'll never forget them.

FIONA, CELEBRITY CHEF

We should all be careful not to judge
others simply by the way they *look*.
Sometimes the scariest-looking creatures
can be the kindest and best of all.

DIANE, SUPREME COURT JUDGE

So, can ALL these chickens be **CRAZY?**

Or are those

HORRIFYING CREATURES

actually . . . trying to do good?

Are they out there doing good deeds?

Or are they **LURKING OUTSIDE YOUR DOOR**, waiting for a chance to show us that they're nothing but a bunch of . . .

. . . BAD GUYS?!

· CHAPTER 1 ·
IF YOU GO DOWN TO
THE WOODS TODAY . . .

Great! So, let's go over the plan ONE MORE TIME.

If you tell us the plan one more time, I'm going to bite you on the butt.

WE KNOW THE PLAN!

Hey! Take it easy, Mr. Snake. This is important.

So anyway . . . I got an **ANONYMOUS CALL** telling me that way out here in **THE WOODS**, there's a bunch of **BULLDOZERS** getting ready to smash up the homes of a lot of **CUTE, FURRY ANIMALS**.

And we're here to make sure

THAT DOESN'T HAPPEN.

WE KNOW ALREADY!

Oh man . . . I don't feel good AT ALL . . .

MR. SHARK!

What?

Where's your disguise?

Oh yeah.
I forgot.

See?! **THIS** is why I
keep repeating the plan!

Yeah, yeah.
Whatevs.

Hey! Who's
THAT guy?!

**WE KNOW THE PLAN!**

Uh-oh. Stop the car . . .

WE'VE BEEN OVER IT A **MILLION** TIMES AND WE **KNOW THE PLAN!**

STOP THE CAR!

**SCREEECH!**

What's wrong?!

Where are YOU going?

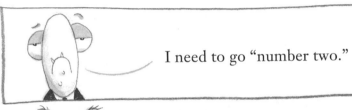

I need to go "number two."

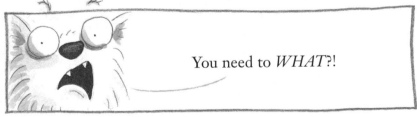

You need to *WHAT*?!

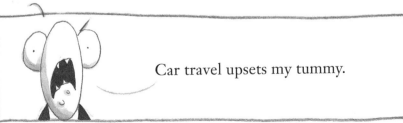

Car travel upsets my tummy.

Are you serious?!
The bulldozers are

RIGHT THERE!

Start without me.
I shouldn't be too long.

Well . . . if you've gotta go . . .

You got it.
If anything moves within
1,000 yards, I'll see it.

All right.
It's time to
be HEROES.

Do you have to say
that EVERY time?

LET'S ROCK!

My car!

LEGS!

Hey, does anyone else think the ground feels weird?

• CHAPTER 2 •
the LAIR OF
DR. MARMALADE

Wha . . . ?

Well, HELLO, genius.
Nice of you to join us . . .

Wait a minute! I know you!

You're that cute little
guinea pig from the old
house next to Sunnyside . . .
You're MARMALADE!

That's **DOCTOR**
Marmalade to you!

Forgive me.

Allow me to
introduce myself . . .

Billionaire mad scientist?!
He's a **GUINEA PIG!**

So what?! Just because I'm a guinea pig, I CAN'T BE A

BILLIONAIRE MAD SCIENTIST?

Oh. Well, no . . . I suppose you could be . . .

Yeah, that's right! And you blew up my awesome car. Why would you do that if you weren't **CRAZY?**

Well, let me think.

Hmmm, yes. Tell me . . . Did you think you could just **BREAK INTO** one of my **CHICKEN FARMS** and steal **10,000 CHICKENS** and I'd just be

COOL WITH THAT?!

Hang on. Are you saying that you blew up our car and strung us up **JUST** because we rescued those chickens?

 FINALLY! Yes, that's right.

But you're *not* mad about all the **BAD** stuff we've done in our lives?

No.

 So that means . . .

THE ONLY REASON WE'RE IN THIS MESS IS BECAUSE OF YOUR STUPID OBSESSION WITH **BEING A HERO!**

What? So this is all **MY** fault now?

OF COURSE IT IS! THE ONLY REASON THIS **CRAZY** GUINEA PIG HAS TIED US UP IS BECAUSE YOU **KEEP MAKING US DO GOOD!**

You really want to fight about this NOW?

I think you have failed to notice my beautiful new toy. Isn't it LOVELY?

Cool. A big red button. What's it do?

Oh, nothing much . . .

It's just going to **DESTROY YOU** and help me **TAKE OVER THE ENTIRE WORLD!** HE HE HE HE HE!

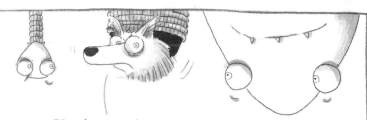

You know what?
I don't think I like that guinea pig.

CHAPTER 3

DO YOU SEE WHAT I SEE?

Hey! *Chicos!*
Where is everybody?
It's not my fault I
needed to poop!

VOOMP!

Shhh!

¡Ay, caramba! What happened to you?!

I jumped from the car one millisecond before it was **BLOWN TO PIECES BY A LASER CANNON** and then I watched the rest of the gang get **SUCKED INTO THE BOWELS OF THE EARTH.**

Oh. Cool.

WHAT?!

It was a **TRAP**, Mr. Piranha.
The bulldozers weren't real. I think
someone got us out here deliberately
and I think Wolf and the guys have
been **CAPTURED!**

My *chicos*!
But where could they be?!

Look over there . . .

Sunnyside?!
But what's a chicken farm doing out here in the middle of the woods?

Exactly!
Fishy, don't you think?

Hey! Who are you calling "Fishy"?
And yes, I DO think.

Um . . . OK. Anyway . . .
We need to get inside that building, and I have a plan . . .

Give us a kiss.

FAINT!

Wow. He's out cold. You really do freak everyone out, don't you?

Yep. Always have . . .

. . . always . . . will . . .

Hey!

What?

I think . . . I just saw . . .

. . . a **NINJA!**

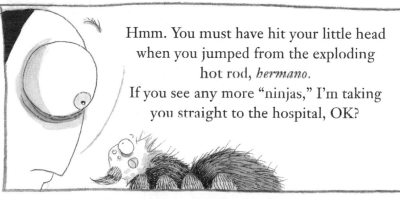

Hmm. You must have hit your little head when you jumped from the exploding hot rod, *hermano*.
If you see any more "ninjas," I'm taking you straight to the hospital, OK?

Because I don't know what we'll find in here, *chico*. But I'll promise you one thing . . .

· CHAPTER 4 ·
the MIND OF A MONSTER

So! Now that I have your attention, I'm going to tell you a little story.

Once upon a time,
there was an itty, bitty guinea pig who got

SICK

of everyone saying how
CUTE and **CUDDLY** he was.

So he decided to do something about it . . .

First of all, he made billions of dollars putting chickens in cages, but somehow that just wasn't enough.

SO! He created a **SECRET WEAPON** that would make sure **NO ONE EVER** called him **CUTE** and **CUDDLY** again. A weapon **SO POWERFUL** that it would change the world forever with the push of a button . . .

THIS BUTTON!

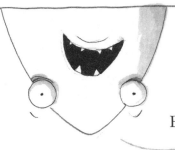

But what's wrong with being
cute and cuddly?
I wish *I* were cute and cuddly!
Everyone **LOVES** guinea pigs.

I don't want *love*,
you ridiculous fish.

I WANT POWER.

And now that I have it, there's

NOTHING

any of you can do to take it away
from me!

HEHE
HEHEHE!

Ahhh . . . sorry. Can you
just give us a second?

What?
Um . . . all right.
But don't take long, OK?

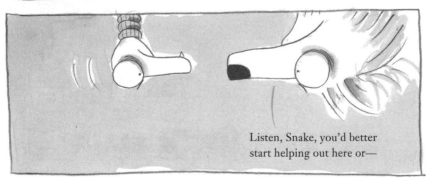

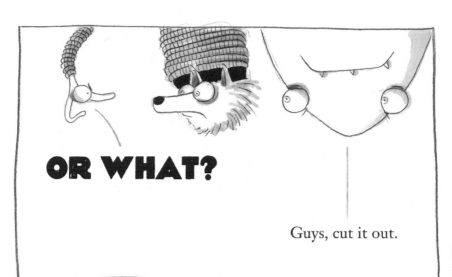

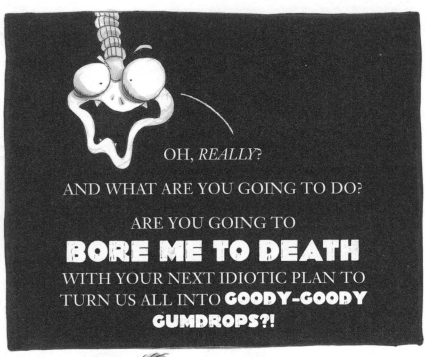

You both need to stop arguing. It's starting to really UPSET me . . .

Warning, schmorning! Do your worst, you dimwitted **HERO WANNABE!**

THAT'S IT!

DON'T DO IT, WOLF.

TOO LATE!

MUNCH!

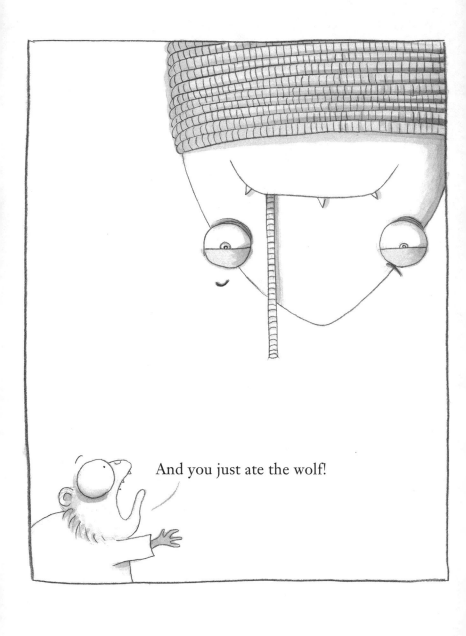

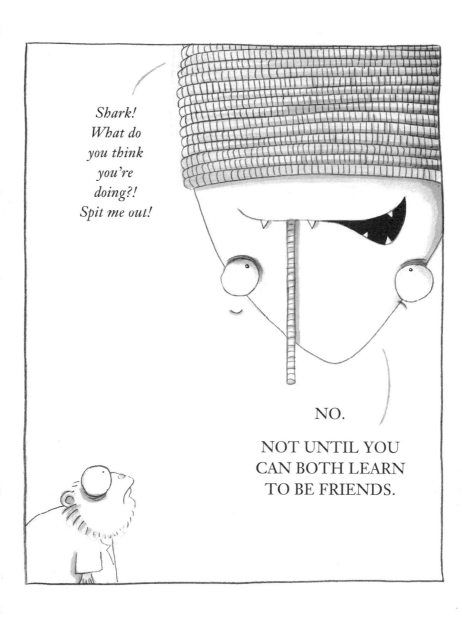

I'm warning you, Wolf! Cough me up!

Not a chance, Slimy.
Shark! I'm NOT going to ask you again!

Wait a minute! Are you inside the shark?!

None of your business!

But that means I'm inside a wolf AND a shark!

Tell someone who cares!

This is like being trapped inside some kind of really disgusting nesting doll and I DON'T LIKE IT!

Big whoop.
Shark, I'm going to count to ten . . .

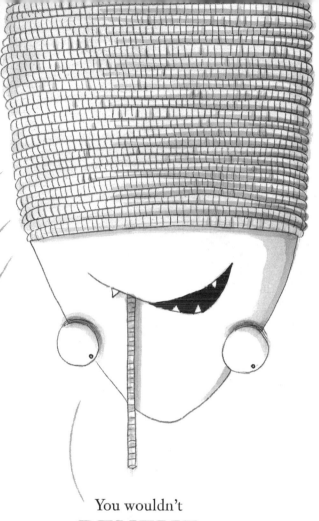

You wouldn't

BELIEVE

what I have to put up with.

· CHAPTER 5 ·
SURPRISE, SURPRISE

NO ONE TIES UP MY *CHICOS* AND GETS AWAY WITH IT! LET'S CUT THAT ROPE **RIGHT NOW!**

NIBBLE!

NIBBLE! NIBBLE!

Mr. Piranha?

Yeah, kid? What is it?

NIBBLE! NIBBLE!

I know this sounds crazy . . . but I really do think I saw a ninja.

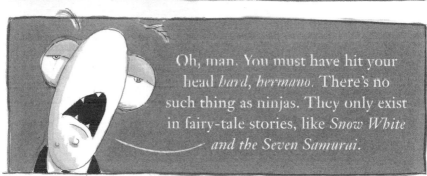

Oh, man. You must have hit your head *hard, hermano.* There's no such thing as ninjas. They only exist in fairy-tale stories, like *Snow White and the Seven Samurai.*

Actually, I'm pretty sure that's not true . . .

FREEZE!

If you don't mind me saying, you seem like a very troubled guinea pig.

 You have NO idea.

 **NOW LET'S GET THIS PARTY STARTED!**

PIRANHA! RUN!

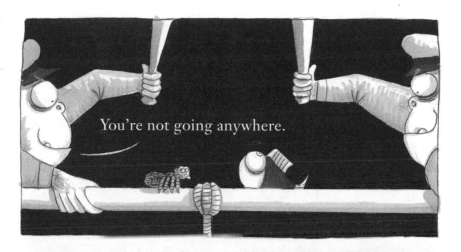

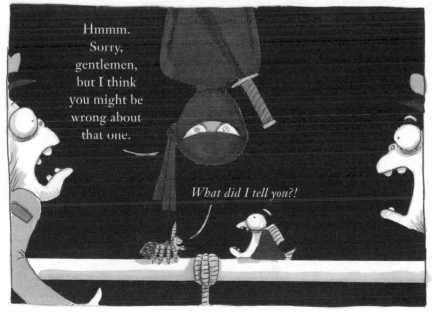

He cut the rope!

SPLURT!

Squeak!

OK. Does someone
want to tell me what's
going on here?

Certainly, Mr. Wolf . . .

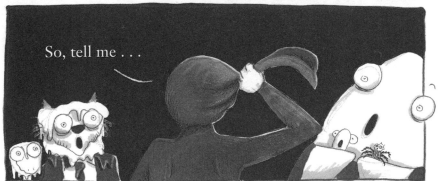

• CHAPTER 6 •
the SECRET AGENT

Who **ARE** you?

My name is
SPECIAL AGENT FOX,
Mr. Shark.
And I'm very pleased
to meet you.

I'm afraid you boys have stumbled into a very dangerous situation.

Doctor Rupert Marmalade is one of the most **DESPICABLE VILLAINS** on the face of the earth. We've been on his tail for years, trying to catch him in the act.

It seems we've finally done it.

We? Who's *we*?

I'm an agent for the

INTERNATIONAL LEAGUE OF HEROES.

We're a secret global organization sworn to protect the earth from evil.

And that is what we do.

Hey! That's kind of what *we* do, isn't it, Wolfie?

We are the . . .
Good Guys Club,
Agent Fox . . .
at your service . . .
heh heh heh . . .
ah . . . yup . . .
gughhhh . . .

The "Good
Guys Club"?
Is that what you
call yourselves?

Yep. We sat up ALL NIGHT
trying to think of the
STUPIDEST NAME in
the HISTORY OF **STUPID**
NAMES and—**BAM!**—
there it was.

Oh, I don't know.
I think it's kind of cute.

But I'm afraid you're a little
out of your depth here, boys.

Your antics at the chicken farm made old Doctor Marmalade here

OBSESSED

with you. But don't worry. We'll soon have him safely locked up, won't we, Marma—

Oh dear.

Has anyone seen where the supervillain went?

Right here, Agent Fox.

Whoops. That's unfortunate.

And I DO hope you enjoy the **END OF THE WORLD!**

He he!

CLUNK!

MY **SECRET WEAPON** HAS BEEN RELEASED AND IT'S **ON ITS WAY!** CAN YOU GUESS WHAT IT IS?

Oh, and just to
make things a little
more interesting . . .

FOOF!

THIS BUILDING WILL
SELF-DESTRUCT
IN 90 SECONDS . . .
89! 88!
87! 86!

Hmm. The old disappearing-up-a-great-big-bendy-tube trick. That's disappointing.

76! 75! 74! 73!

Well, the building is about to blow and we have seconds to live. Any ideas, gentlemen?

· CHAPTER 7 ·
LEARNING TO RIDE A BIKE

Climb aboard, everyone, and I'll get you out of here.

We won't all fit on one motorcycle!

Hmm. You could be right. I don't suppose any of you can ride one of these . . . ?

Yep!

You can?

Yeeeah.

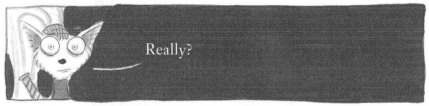

Really?

Nnnnn . . . *yeeeeah.*

Wow. You have a very unusual style, Mr. Wolf. Very impressive.

But I'm afraid things are going to be a little more difficult than we thought.

Oh, really? Why's that?

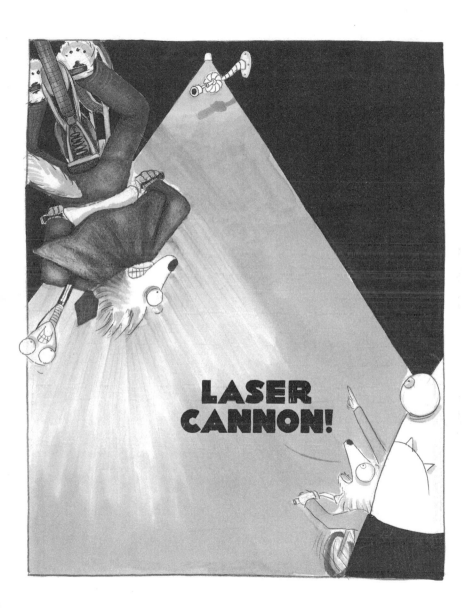

Wow. He really is awfully brave, isn't he?

Well, yes. In Bolivia, we have a name for people like that . . .

We call them "idiots."

I HATE YOU, WOLF!

WELL, I **DON'T** HATE YOU, SNAKE!

AND I **WON'T GIVE UP ON YOU**, NO MATTER WHAT HAPPENS.

I'M SORRY I **ATE** YOU EARLIER. BUT I'M **NOT** SORRY FOR GETTING YOU INTO ALL THIS TROUBLE.

THIS IS WHAT HEROES DO.

AND I TRULY BELIEVE **YOU HAVE A HERO INSIDE YOU**, MR. SNAKE.

AND I'LL NEVER STOP BELIEVING THAT. **EVER.**

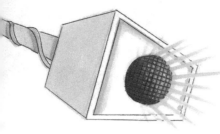

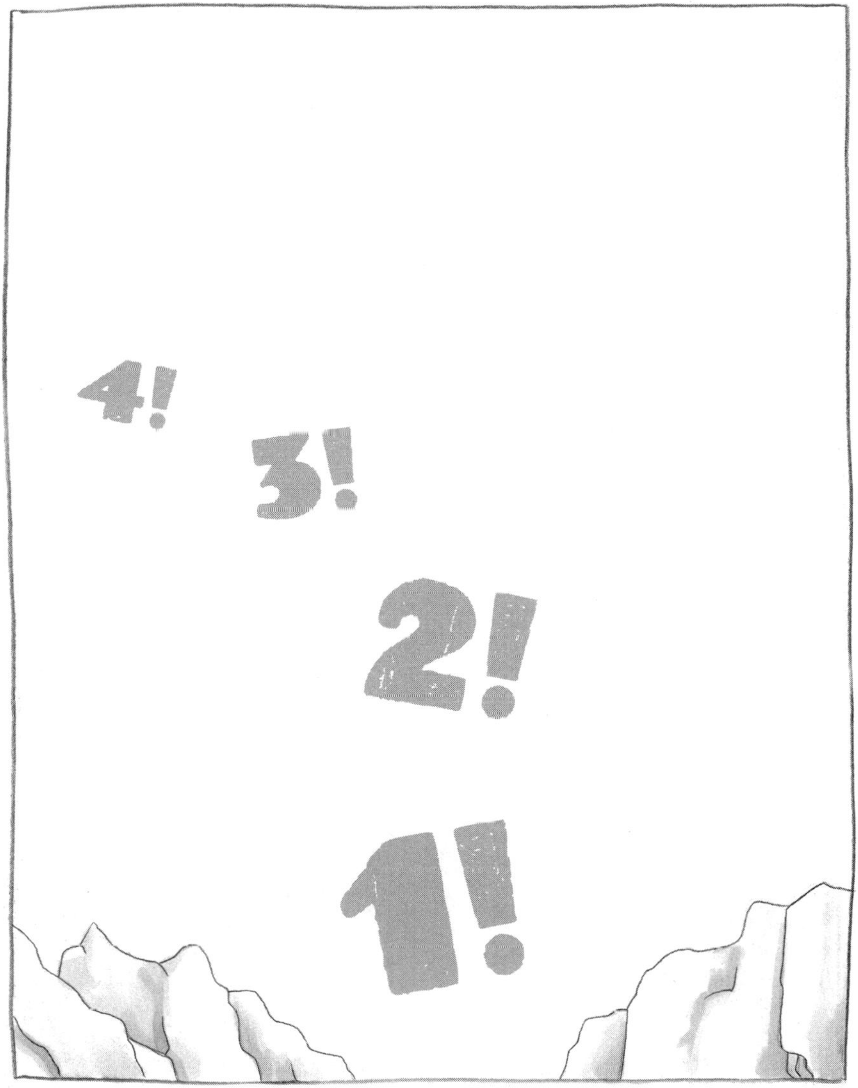
4!
3!
2!
1!

· CHAPTER 8 ·
A LITTLE FAVOR

What happened?
Did we blow up?
Is this . . . heaven?

It can't be.
You're here.

HEHEHEHE!

Tricked you!
The building wasn't
REALLY going to blow up!

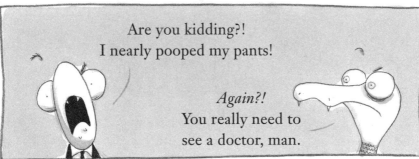

Are you kidding?!
I nearly pooped my pants!

Again?!
You really need to
see a doctor, man.

YOU DIDN'T
REALLY THINK
I'D BLOW UP MY
**SECRET
WEAPON**,
DID YOU?

I'm getting sick of this.
WHAT secret weapon?
I'll bet it's just another trick!

Hmmm.
Well, you just wait a few minutes,
Mr. Wolf, and see what comes out
of this tunnel!

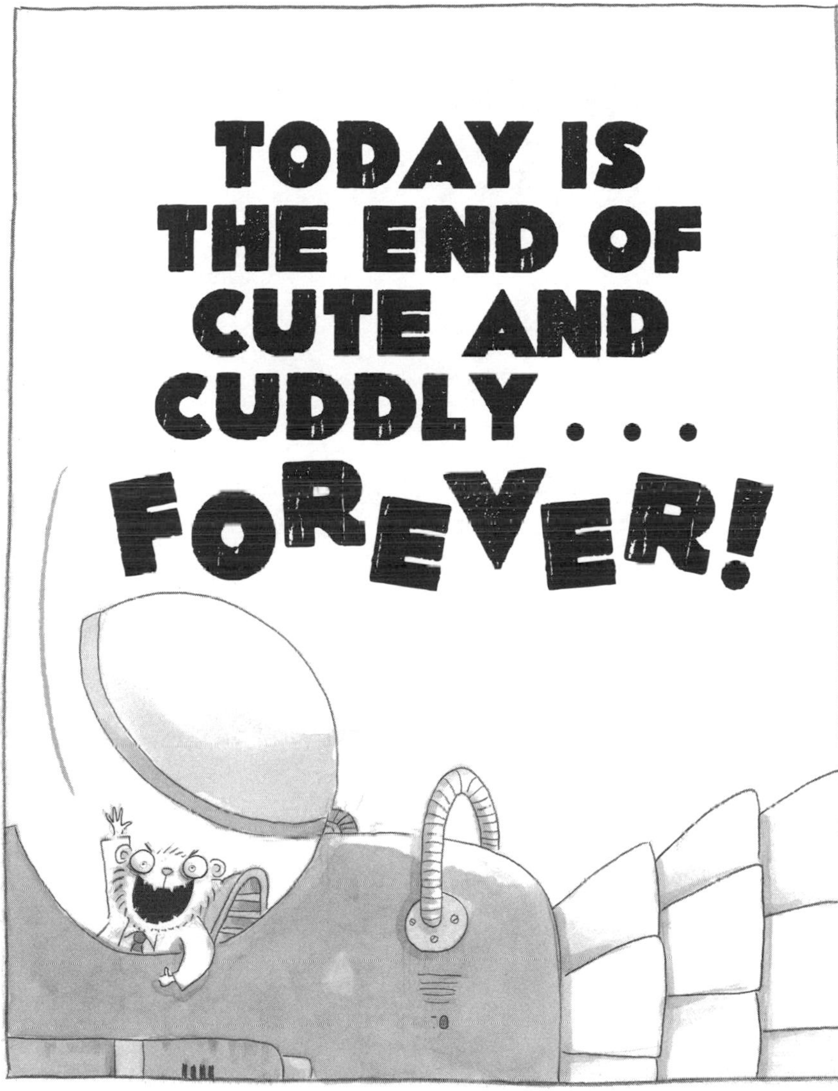
TODAY IS THE END OF CUTE AND CUDDLY . . .
FOREVER!

I really don't like that guinea pig.

Nor do I, Mr. Wolf.
And that's why I need
to ask you a favor.

Anything!

I need to follow
Marmalade
RIGHT NOW.
But someone
needs to stay here
and deal with his
**SECRET
WEAPON**.

Any minute now, something **TRULY TERRIFYING** will come out of that tunnel and I need some heroes to be standing guard when it does.

Will **YOU** be my heroes, gentlemen?

 Will you help me

SAVE THE WORLD?

 Um . . . I'm really not sure . . .

 I actually have a hair appointment to get to . . .

 I'd love to help, *señorita*, but I'm afraid I need to find a clean pair of pants . . .

 Sister, you're out of your mind . . .

Yes, there are quite a few perks to being a hero, Mr. Wolf.

Oh, and Mr. Snake?

Yeah?

I know what you did at
the chicken farm.
YOU are the reason
those chickens are free.
You're ALREADY a hero.

You just have to
start *believing* it.

Good luck, boys!

ZOOOOM!

· CHAPTER 9 ·
CUTE AND CUDDLY NO MORE

Are you guys ready for this?

NO.

Fair enough.
I'm not sure I am either.
But it doesn't matter,
does it? Because we have
a job to do. It's up to us
to protect the world.

It's up to us—
**THE GOOD
GUYS CLUB.**

Seriously, man, now that we've heard about the **INTERNATIONAL LEAGUE OF HEROES**, our name sounds so lame it makes me wish I had hands—so I could **SLAP YOU**.

Really?
You don't like our name?

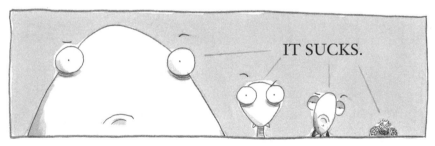

IT SUCKS.

OK . . . well . . .
We **ARE** helping the
awesome League of
Heroes, right now . . .

So that kind of makes us awesome, too, doesn't it?

Kind of.

Well then, Kind-of-Awesome-League-of-Good-Guys-Guys, let's show this SECRET WEAPON what we're made of!

Hey! **HAHAHAHA!**
Everybody relax!
LOOK!
IT'S JUST ANOTHER **TRICK!**
IT'S JUST A BUNCH OF . . .

Phew!
Well, **THAT'S** a relief!

No, no, no . . . wait a minute . . .
There's something **WEIRD**
about those kittens.
Why are they **LIMPING?**
And **MOANING?**
And . . . **DROOLING?**

NO!
IT CAN'T BE!
IT IS!
IT'S . . .
IT'S AN ARMY
OF . . .

ZOMBIE KITTENS!

It's a **ZOMBIE KITTEN APOCALYPSE!**

Should you **panic**? Should you **cry**?

Should you **poop your pants**?

NO! You should sit back and watch the **FUR FLY** as the world's **BADDEST GOOD GUYS** take on **MAD MARMALADE'S MEOWING MONSTERS!**

You'll **laugh till you cry**. Or **laugh till you fart**. (It doesn't matter which, it's totally your choice.)

Just don't miss . . . *the BAD GUYS in Attack of the Zittens!*

THE BADNESS CONTINUES!

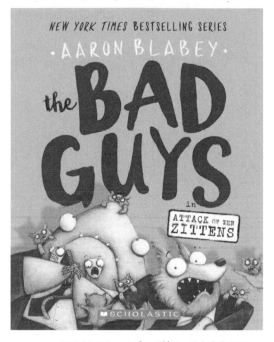

NEW YORK TIMES BESTSELLING SERIES

·AARON BLABEY·

the BAD GUYS

in

ATTACK OF THE ZITTENS

SCHOLASTIC

#4: ATTACK OF THE ZITTENS

CAN THE BAD GUYS SAVE THE WORLD FROM EVIL DR. MARMALADE'S MEOWING MONSTERS?!? THEY'LL NEED HELP FROM FOXY AGENT FOX, A SWAMPY SECRET ZOMBIE ANTIDOTE, AND THE FEISTIEST, TOOTHIEST, HUNGRIEST GRANNY AROUND. GET READY TO WATCH THE FUR FLY!

NEW YORK TIMES BESTSELLING SERIES

·AARON BLABEY·

the BAD GUYS

in INTERGALACTIC GAS

■SCHOLASTIC

#5: INTERGALACTIC GAS

THE BAD NEWS? THE WORLD IS ENDING. THE GOOD NEWS? THE BAD GUYS ARE BACK TO SAVE IT! SURE, THEY MIGHT HAVE TO "BORROW" A ROCKET. AND MR. PIRANHA *MIIIIIGHT* HAVE EATEN TOO MANY BEAN BURRITOS. SURVIVING THIS MISSION MAY ONLY BE ONE SMALL STEP FOR MAN, BUT IT'S ONE GIANT LEAP FOR THE BAD GUYS.

#6: ALIEN VS. BAD GUYS

THE BAD GUYS ARE VANISHING! A CREATURE WITH *TONS* OF TEETH AND *WAY* TOO MANY BUTTS IS STEALING THEM, ONE BY ONE. IS THIS THE END FOR THE BAD GUYS? MAYBE. WILL IT BE FUNNY? YOU BET YOUR BUTTS IT WILL!

#7: DO-YOU-THINK-HE-SAURUS?!

IT'S THE DAWN OF TIME, AND NOTHING CAN RIVAL THE TERRIFYING POWER OF THE DINOSAURS. EXCEPT MAYBE THAT WOLF OVER THERE. THE ONE NEXT TO THE SNAKE AND THE SHARK AND THAT SARDINEY-LOOKING THING. HUH?! THE BAD GUYS HAVE GONE BACK IN TIME! THIS IS *ALL* WRONG. THIS IS *ALL* BAD. THIS IS *ALL* AWESOME!

NEW YORK TIMES BESTSELLING SERIES
· AARON BLABEY ·

the BAD GUYS

in SUPERBAD

SCHOLASTIC

#8: SUPERBAD

HEROES WANTED! BUT WHAT IS THE INTERNATIONAL LEAGUE OF HEROES LOOKING FOR EXACTLY? GIGANTIC MUSCLES? ATOMIC SPEED? PSYCHIC POWERS? SHAPE-SHIFTING AWESOMENESS? POSSIBLY. BUT DO THEY WANT THE BAD GUYS, WHOSE SUPERPOWERS ARE SUPER UNRELIABLE? DUH! WHY WOULD YOU EVEN ASK THAT?!

#9: THE BIG BAD WOLF

THE SKY GOES DARK. THE CITY TREMBLES. THE SCREAMS BEGIN . . . AND EVERYONE'S FAVORITE WOLF HAS *A LOT* OF EXPLAINING TO DO. HE'S *BIG*? YEP. *BAD*? YOU BETCHA. UNMISSABLE? *YESSSSSSSSSSSSS*. HIDE UNDER A TABLE AND STRAP ON A HELMET – THE BIG BAD WOLF IS READY TO BLOW!